nickelodeon
TEENAGE MUTANT NINJA TURTLES

HOW TO BE A NINJA

Chris Conti

sourcebooks
jabberwocky

WELCOME. I AM Master Splinter. I have devoted my long life to the ancient art of *ninjutsu*. For many years now, I have been *sensei* to a great team of warriors: my sons. Teaching them these ancient skills and guiding them as they have come of age has been the greatest honor of my life.

In this book, I have gathered all of my wisdom. These are the lessons you will need to become a force for good in the world. But like any devoted teacher, I know that the master can also learn from the student! My sons and their loyal friends also have just as much to teach as I do, and so you will hear from them, too.

Remember: in order to become a warrior on the outside, you must first master the warrior within. Do this, and you will bring honor to the ninja, to me, and to yourself.

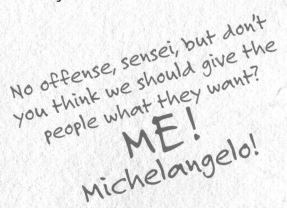

No offense, sensei, but don't you think we should give the people what they want? ME! Michelangelo!

TRADITION

ALL YOUNG STUDENTS of the ninja arts develop their own style. As you study these skills, you will come to learn what is special and unique about you.

But never forget that the way of the ninja, though known to just a few, has a long tradition. This tradition can be summed up in one word: secrecy. Over the centuries, every ninja has learned from a master how to move in silence, hide from sight, travel quickly over any obstacle, and wield his or her chosen weapon.

The kicks, punches, and weapon strikes of a martial artist are all well and good, but it is the ability to surprise and confuse your enemy that is at the very core of being a ninja. First you must learn this ancient tradition of secrecy, and then you must develop your unique style. Only then can you become a true ninja master.

LESSON 2

DISCIPLINE

HI, MY NAME is Leonardo, and I'm the leader of the Teenage Mutant Ninja Turtles. For me, the most important skill of all is discipline. You may be talented, but you can't become truly great unless you focus and work hard. Being truly great doesn't just mean defeating your enemy, it also means making time to chill out with your family and friends!

You might be the leader, but I, Michelangelo, was born with a rare natural awesomeness!

I know that Master Splinter looks to me as the most disciplined of his students. And one day, I hope to become the worthy leader he sees in me. If you practice hard enough, you can master anything. And not just ninja skills. This is true for anything you want to accomplish!

LESSON 3
STRENGTH

RAPHAEL HERE. MASTER Splinter asked me to write this because he knows that for me, strength is what it's all about. Nothing makes my *sai* more effective than a big arm to swing it! My muscle is my real weapon. But *sensei* always reminds me that the ninja's greatest strength is strength of mind. When I focus my strength and control my temper, that's when I'm unstoppable.

Two words:
Hot. Head.
Two more words:
Chill. Out.

Splinter keeps telling me that if a strong warrior is to stand for good, then he must know when it is time to be gentle. I'm working on it. But it can be pretty hard to stay calm when the Kraang, the Triceratons, or any other bad guys come around. Or when Mikey eats the last slice of pizza...again!

And another two words: Pizza. Mine.

MODERN TECHNOLOGY

MY NAME IS Donatello. As the inventor in the group, I've made a few gadgets that are essential for today's ninja warrior. The Shellraiser. The Turtle Sub. The Patrol Buggy. Ooze Specs, TPod, TPhone, TRawket...oh, Donatello! I love your mind!

VERY LOW TO GROUND

TOP VIEW

GRAPPLING HOOK WINCH SET

Splinter is always reminding me that the true nature of the ninja lies in ancient tradition...but I've got all this fascinating modern knowledge just waiting to be turned into bad guy-busting awesomeness! So I'm learning that the real trick is finding balance between ancient ways and Turtle tech. That's why, along with my inventions, Splinter taught me to use the *bo* staff. When you can blend lessons from the past with ideas of the future, that's when you have the right tools to protect the planet!

I can do science stuff, too.
I'm great at dancing the robot.

LESSON 5
CREATIVITY

YO, WHAT UP, truth seekers? My name is Michelangelo and I am a Turtle of many talents. *Sensei* asked me to teach you about being creative, which is no surprise since I'm the best at naming evil mutants! Snakeweed, Dogpound, Bebop, and Rocksteady...all those names came from my imagination! I bring this level of creativity to everything I do. Breakdancing, skateboarding, pizza concocting, and my seriously rad ninja-ing!

I know I'm awesome, but why would you want to be like someone else when you can be you? That's what creativity is all about, bro. So, you want to be a ninja. Are you super strong? Totally sneaky? Can you draw maps and plan missions? Adding your unique talent to create your own individual style will totally take your opponent by surprise. Shock and awe, dude! Booyakasha!

This guy is a stone cold genius!

LESSON 6

STEALTH

SILENCE AND INVISIBILITY are super-important when it comes to being a ninja. The ability to go unseen, to move without being heard, is probably the most important skill of all!

Especially for us. We have to live our whole lives in secret.

Our weapons and training make us pretty awesome in battle, but when ninjas are effectively concealed from their enemies, they may be able to complete a mission without ever having to resort to fighting at all. Do not mistake the unwillingness to fight as cowardice; the ability to move unseen is the mark of an expert ninja.

If you can sneak up close enough to the bad guys to hear them talk, or to see their plans, then you can figure out how to stop them. But you'd better not get caught! That means you can't let the bad guys hear you or see you sneaking around. Remember to keep quiet, stay in the shadows, and hide behind anything you can find. Complete your mission, and get out of there before they find you!

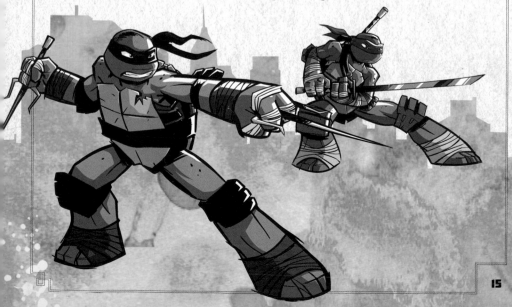

FRIENDSHIP

APRIL O'NEIL

I'M APRIL O'NEIL, and Master Splinter has trusted me to tell you about one of the most important lessons in all of your ninja training. In my time with the Ninja Turtles, I have learned there is only one force greater than that of a master ninja: a team of trusted friends. When you have a whole team working together—no matter how different you are from one another—you can accomplish anything.

CASEY JONES

HEY, STUDENTS. THIS class is Pain 101 and I'm your instructor, Casey Jones. Just kidding! I typically fly solo, but being part of a group like the Turtles has changed my life. I've got their back and they've got mine. Being able to rely on yourself is great, but being part of a team is the sickest thing in the world! Goongala!

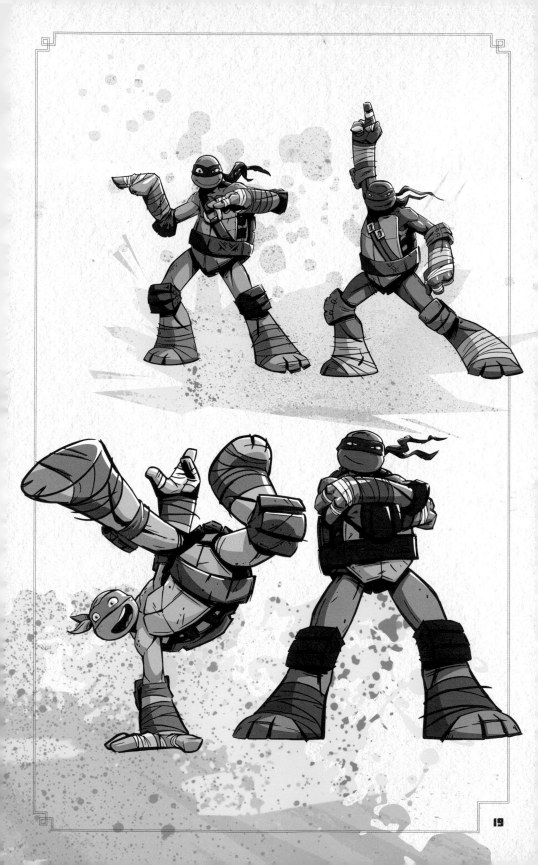

KARAI
a.k.a. Hamato Miwa

MY NAME IS Karai. I was once an enemy of the Turtles, raised by Shredder to believe Splinter was responsible for my mother's death. But eventually I discovered the truth: that Splinter and the Turtles are my true family and that family is your greatest strength.

LESSON 8

TEAMWORK

WHETHER YOU ARE moving silently across rooftops, speeding through the sewer, or sneaking into an enemy hideout, working as a team is the key to success. If you focus only on your individual talents and goals, you will find it impossible to achieve the victory you seek.

Four shells are better than one!

Nowhere is teamwork more important than in combat. Every strike, every block, every move you make is stronger with a trusted friend at your side. You can always look forward with confidence when you know your friends have your back.

Trust that your family and friends will always be there for you, and show them that you are loyal to them as well.

MY NEW STUDENT, you are well on your way to becoming a ninja. My sons and their trusted friends have shown you the path of the hero. But in order to defeat your enemies, you must first understand them.

Study the following pages carefully. Your foes will stop at nothing to fulfill their evil plans. But when you know what lies inside their hearts, you can predict their actions and defeat them at every turn.

Looks like playtime's over. Hang on to your shells!

KNOW YOUR ENEMY

THE KRAANG

THE ALIEN BEINGS known as the Kraang are brain-like creatures who use their brilliant minds to try to take over the world. They cannot survive in Earth's atmosphere. They want to transform it so they can live here...but doing so would wipe out all of humanity.

They see themselves as heroes and explorers, but in truth they are the opposite. Rather than using their great powers to protect others, they are plotting to destroy our world and take it for themselves.

Though they are intelligent creatures, their bodies are weak and frail. For this reason, direct attack is often best against the Kraang. Work as a team. Overtake them with force. Surprise them by jumping out of the shadows. Make them afraid and you can defeat them.

THE FOOT CLAN

BEWARE! THERE IS a vast army of ninja warriors working against good. They are known as
the Foot Clan. Originally from Japan, they are
fearless fighters who obey Shredder without
question. They move silently through the
shadows of the city wearing identical black
uniforms. The Foot Clan come from all walks
of life and often plot and fight in their civilian
identities as well.

FOOTBOTS

CREATED BY THE Kraang, Footbots are robots that are programmed to fight for the evil Shredder using over 900 different styles of combat. Not only are they faster and stronger than people, but they are also able to learn new moves during a fight. This means you must never repeat your moves when you face them. You must remain unpredictable in order to be victorious.

BEBOP
a.k.a. Anton Zeck

BEBOP AND ROCKSTEADY are mutated, streetwise tough guys who use their strength and fierce nature for their own selfish gain. They are powerful but unskilled in the true art of combat. You can defeat them with a disciplined attack.

ROCKSTEADY
a.k.a. Ivan Steranko

RAHZAR
a.k.a. Chris Bradford

RAHZAR WAS ONCE one of Shredder's top henchmen. Now mutated, he also fights with fierce teeth and claws. Use your defensive moves against him. Wait for the perfect time to strike.

THE RAT KING
a.k.a. Victor Falco

THE RAT KING is a former scientist who telepathically commands an army of rats, making him a most difficult opponent to defeat. Jump to high ground. Use billboards, power lines, and water towers as your means of defense. Go anywhere the rat army cannot follow.

TIGER CLAW
a.k.a. Takeshi

TIGER CLAW IS an assassin and bounty hunter who is skilled in the fighting arts. Half man, half tiger, he was mutated by the Kraang and trained by Shredder. When facing him in battle, remember that your weapons can be used to block, not only to strike. Keep moving. Wait for him to show an opening.

NEWTRALIZER

NEWTRALIZER IS THE arch-enemy of the Kraang, but he's no good guy, either. He can catch and squeeze enemies with his strong tail, and his thick skin protects him from even the fiercest weapon attacks. Speed is critical when facing him. Use your jumps and flips to avoid his tail. Attack as a team.

SNAKEWEED
a.k.a. Snake

SNAKEWEED WAS ONCE a human thug working for the Kraang. After being splashed with Mutagen, he turned into a twelve-foot-tall plant mutant. Not only is he huge and powerful, but he also blames the Turtles for his mutation. Use his size against him by hiding in small spaces. Use his anger against him by keeping him mad and out of control. But be careful. Snakeweed's strength and evil nature cannot be taken lightly.

SPIDER BYTEZ
a.k.a. Vic

WITH MANY CLAWS, spider webbing, and even acid spit, Spider Bytez has fierce weapons and an angry temper. This opponent should not be faced alone. Attack from many sides at once, and use all your weapons to challenge this foe. Keep a cool head and this will give you the advantage you need.

SHREDDER
a.k.a. Oroku Saki

SHREDDER IS THE leader of the nefarious Foot Clan. He was known as Oroku Saki when he lived in Japan. It was there that he ripped my family apart! Ruthless and twisted, Shredder wants nothing more than to take us down once and for all. You will need to remember all of your training in order to stand a chance against Shredder. Most important, you must rely on one another, for only together do you have any hope of defeating this criminal overlord.

NINJA MISSION #1

STEALTH

THE PLAN

YOUR ASSIGNMENT: LOCATE a family member in your home. Move in silence to a position that is as close to them as possible without being detected. Observe their movements and actions. Then, retreat back to your team and report your observations.

This skill is very hard to master, and you may not succeed on your first attempt. If you are detected, simply act like nothing unusual is happening. Keeping your assignment a secret is part of your training. Then, keep trying. Only through practice will you improve. This is true of everything in life.

NINJA MISSION #2

TEAMWORK

AT SOME POINT in the future, you may be required to plant a sensor or listening device inside an enemy location. In order to complete such a mission, you will need to display exceptional teamwork.

You must find a trusted partner to help you on this mission. Perhaps a parent or another family member will be willing to assist you. With your partner, locate a family member in your home. Tell your partner to walk up to this person and engage them in simple, friendly conversation. While your partner is talking, sneak into the area and place an object as close to the target person as possible. A perfect object to use for this mission is this book itself. If there is a table or seat nearby, try to place this book there, and then retreat undetected.

Your partner will notice your movements, and they will know when it is time to end the conversation and meet back at another location.

Then, it is your turn to walk up to your target person. Ask them, "Have you seen my Ninja Turtle Training Book? Oh, here it is!" Then simply pick up the book and walk away. If your target didn't notice you place the book near them, you have completed your mission!

MY FRIEND, THIS concludes our teachings. Return to this book often as you continue to sharpen your skills. Loyalty is a gift; if you are helpful to your family and friends, they will always be there to help you as well.

Never forget that what makes you different from all others is also what makes you *special*. No one in the world can do exactly what you can do.

I'm not cryin', dude! I've just got something in my eye! All this emotion reminds me of PIZZA!

Published by Sourcebooks, Inc.
P.O. Box 4410, Naperville, Illinois 60567-4410
(630) 961-3900
Fax: (630) 961-2168
sourcebooks.com

Source of Production: Leo Paper, Heshan City,
Guangdong Province, China
Date of Production: August 2017
Run Number: 5010196

Printed and bound in China.
LEO 10 9 8 7 6 5 4 3 2 1